How Emily Blair Got Her Fabulous Hair

by Susan Garrison

Pictures by Marjorie Priceman

BridgeWater Paperback

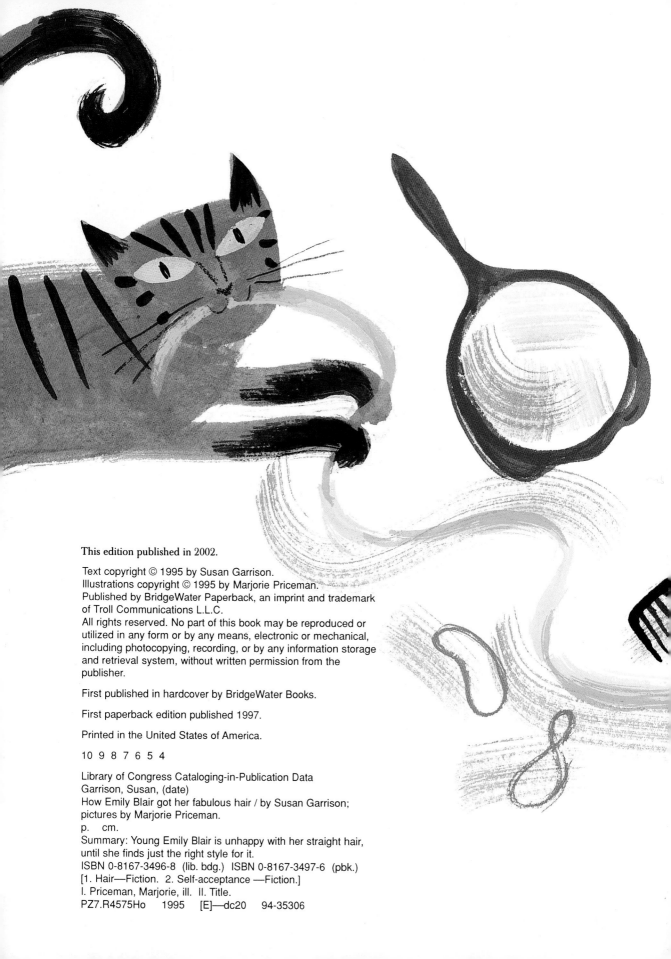

This edition published in 2002.

Text copyright © 1995 by Susan Garrison.
Illustrations copyright © 1995 by Marjorie Priceman.
Published by BridgeWater Paperback, an imprint and trademark
of Troll Communications L.L.C.

First published in hardcover by BridgeWater Books.

First paperback edition published 1997.

Printed in the United States of America.

10 9 8 7 6 5 4

Library of Congress Cataloging-in-Publication Data
Garrison, Susan, (date)
How Emily Blair got her fabulous hair / by Susan Garrison;
pictures by Marjorie Priceman.
p.   cm.
Summary: Young Emily Blair is unhappy with her straight hair,
until she finds just the right style for it.
ISBN 0-8167-3496-8 (lib. bdg.) ISBN 0-8167-3497-6 (pbk.)
[1. Hair—Fiction. 2. Self-acceptance —Fiction.]
I. Priceman, Marjorie, ill. II. Title.
PZ7.R4575Ho   1995   [E]—dc20   94-35306

To my first hair stylist, my mother.
S.G.

To my long-suffering, straight-haired mother.
M.P.

Emily Blair had very straight hair, and it had been that way forever. When she was born, three straight strands stood on her head like pine needles perched on a peach.

When she was four, she grew more hair that spilled from her head like spaghetti.

When she was five, she tried out her mom's curlers. She coiled and clipped, she wrapped and she rolled the pink foam and black bristles that stung her scalp. But when she unwound each one, she found hairs crinkled and dented and not at all like she expected.

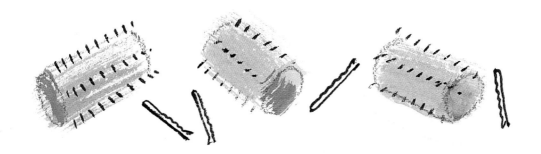

When Emily reached first grade, she made a new friend, named Pamela Paine, whose whole head rippled with golden waves. Together they would play pretend beauty parlor, where Emily Blair would do her most wonderful work on Pamela's hair.

She had a special style for Pamela, the Princess of Permano;

a new hairdo for Pamela, the Mysterious Movie Star;

and all the treasures she kept in her drawer she saved to create

Pamela, the Ambassador of Outer Space!

But Emily Blair still wanted her own curly hair. She tied

tendrils from a grapevine to the top of her head.

She ate an entire plate of carrot curls.

She rubbed heads with a poodle,

made a wish on the tail of a pig, and went right through ten tubes of glue to make a wig of macaroni.

One day Pamela Paine said to Emily, "Today I would like you to make me a braid."

Emily tried to pry Pamela's hair into three equal clumps. She crisscrossed and tucked the pieces into a pattern. But the curls kept on curling and the waves went their own way . . . and Pamela's braid looked dreadful!

"Let me give it a try!" Pamela said. "Let's switch sides!" So Emily passed her the comb and sat down.

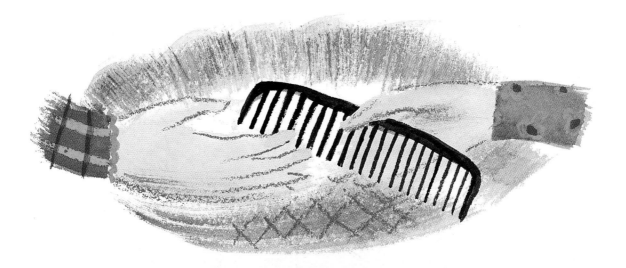

She felt the scratch of the comb as Pamela made three even parts. Pamela crisscrossed and tucked the pieces into a perfect pattern, over-and-under and over-and-under and over-and-under again. Then she finished with a snap of an elastic and a red ribbon tie.

Pamela handed Emily the mirror. Emily saw herself smile as she watched her perfect braid swing side to side every time she turned her head. She reached back to touch every even bump, bump by bump, all the way down to the ribbon.

Emily Blair learned to braid her own hair. She made simple single braids for Emily, the Star Student.

She twisted braids into buns for Madam Blair, the Ballerina.

And with a braid on each side and pieces of lace she could make Emily, the Cowgirl Bride.

Emily Blair loved her very
straight hair . . . and she had
the most fabulous braids in
the entire first grade!